Contents

Chapter One

The No-Pet Problem

Sarah sat at the table.

She looked sad.

Tears ran down her cheeks.

"What's wrong?" asked Mum.

"It's pet day at school next Monday, and I don't have a pet."

"Oh dear," said Mum. "What can we do?"

"Can I get a pet?" asked Sarah.

Mum hugged her.

"Sorry, we don't have room for the kind of pet that you would like."

"But what will I do?" said Sarah.
"Hey, I know! Let's make
a pet!" she said.

"Make a pet?" asked Mum.
"What could we make?"

"A horse!" said Sarah.

"A horse?" replied Mum.

"How can we make a horse?"

"I have an idea," said Sarah.

"Well... OK," said Mum. "We can give it a try. What do we need?"

Sarah and Mum sat at the table and made a list.

wood
nails
paint
wire
glue

Chapter Two

In the Garage

The next day, when Sarah
came home from school,
there was a big piece of wood
in the garage.

Before Dad came home, Sarah
and Mum used pencils and paper
to draw the parts that they
needed to make a horse.

Bobby helped, too.

After dinner, Mum, Dad, and Sarah cut out the pieces of wood using the saw.

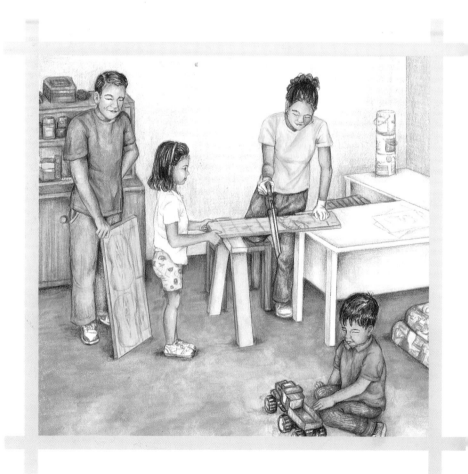

"That's enough work for tonight,"
said Dad. "Rome wasn't built
in a day."

So Sarah went to read a book.

Chapter Three

Teamwork

After dinner the next night,
Sarah and Mum got
a hammer and some nails.
They hammered and banged
the horse together.

"We're getting there," said Mum.
"But, like Dad always says, 'Rome
wasn't built in a day.'"

So Sarah went to draw a picture.

The next day after school,
Mum got some paint
and they painted the horse.
Bobby helped, too.

"Now we have to let the paint
dry," said Bobby.

So Sarah went to ride her bike.

The following night, Sarah
and Dad got some old cloth
material and stuck it onto
the horse's body.

They made the mane and
the tail from some bristly rope.
Sarah stuck on two plastic eyes.

Then Sarah went off to bed.

She gave her pet a hug.

"Goodnight, Horsey," she said.

Chapter Four

Pet Day at School

On Saturday, the whole family
drove out to Uncle Bill's farm.
Sarah had a ride on
one of his big horses.

The whole time, Sarah was thinking about her pet horse. She couldn't wait for pet day on Monday.

At last, Monday morning came.
"Pet day today!" said Sarah,
as she walked to the bus stop,
carrying her horse.

At school, there were dogs,
cats, goldfish, and mice.
There were guinea pigs, rabbits,
a frog, and a lamb. There
was even a chick and a calf.

"Good morning, Sarah,"
said Ms Grant. "Is this your pet?"

"Yes," replied Sarah.
"This is my pet horse."

"What a great pet," said
Ms Grant. "I bet it doesn't eat
much food. Does it have a name?"
Sarah thought for a moment.
"Its name is Rome."
"That's an interesting name,"
said Ms Grant.

Josh said, "That's not a real pet. It's only made of wood. My puppy is a real pet." His puppy barked with excitement.

"So!" said Sarah, and she reached under her horse and flicked a secret switch.

Nnnneeeigh went her horse.

All the children laughed and wanted to play with Sarah's pet.

Sarah told Ms Grant, "Last Saturday, we all went to my Uncle Bill's farm. We rode horses and then we recorded the sounds that horses make. We put Dad's little tape recorder on my horse. When I turn the switch, it plays the horse sounds back."

She flicked the switch again.
It sounded just like Sarah's horse
had made the noises itself!
But, by the end of the day,
her pet could manage only
a weak *Nnnn...*

"It's tired," said Sarah.

The frog won a ribbon for "the Greenest Pet".

The lamb won a ribbon for "the Friskiest Pet".

The chick won a ribbon for "the Cluckiest Pet".

A cat won a ribbon for "the Whiskeriest Pet".

And Sarah's horse won a ribbon for "the Most Popular Pet".

That night, Sarah put her ribbon up on her bedroom wall. Mum made a special cake for dessert.

"We made a great pet," said Mum. "What do you want to make next?"

"Whoa there, Mum," said Sarah, laughing. "Remember, Rome wasn't built in a day!"

From the Author

I once made a model horse for my daughter. She loved it for a while. However, when I suggested that she take it to school for pet day, she did *not* agree that it was a terrific idea!

Alan Whitaker

From the Illustrator

I spent part of my childhood living on a farm and have had many pets. When I was creating the illustrations for *Sarah's Pet*, I drew the characters from real people.

Julia Crouth